W9-AVJ-984

BEAR IN A SQUARE

Written by Stella Blackstone
Illustrated by Debbie Harter

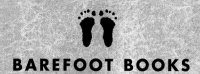

BAREFOOT BOOKS

Find the bear
in the square

Find the hearts
in the queen's hair

Find the circles in the pool

Find the rectangles in the school

Find the moons
in the cave

Find the triangles on the wave

Find the diamonds on the crown

Find the zigzags around the clown

Find the ovals in the park

Find the stars
in the dark

Square

Heart

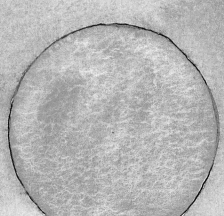

Circle

Rectangle

Moon

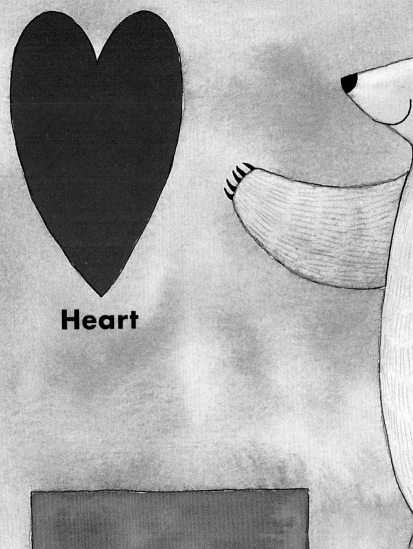

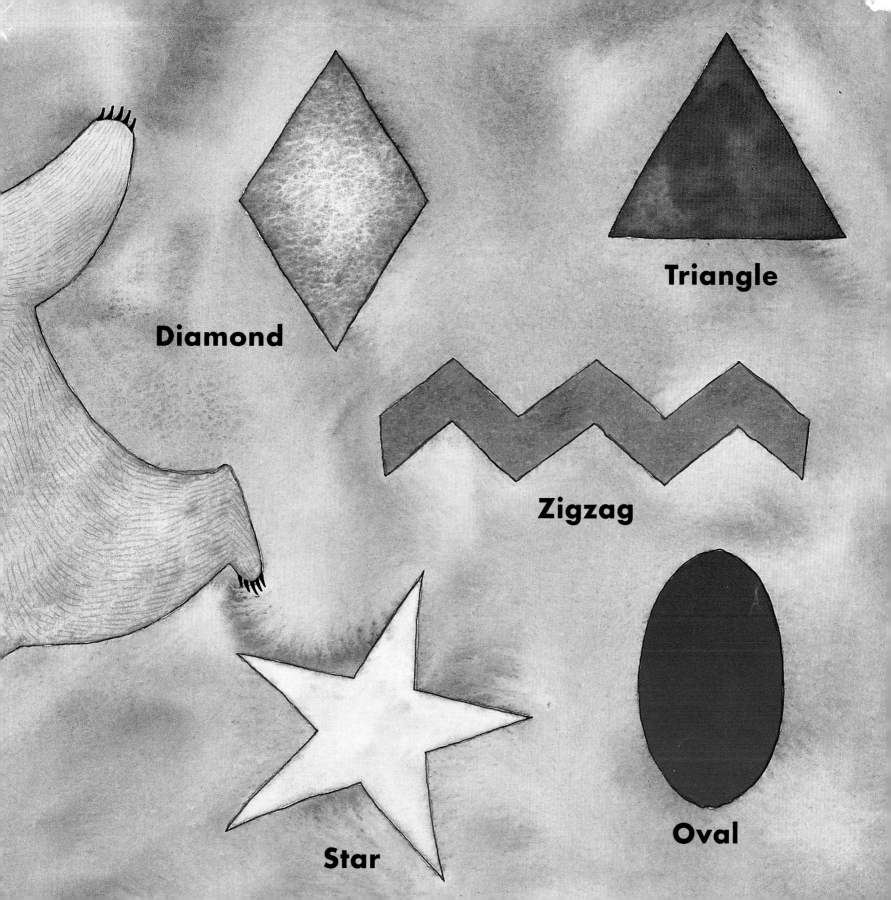

Diamond

Triangle

Zigzag

Star

Oval

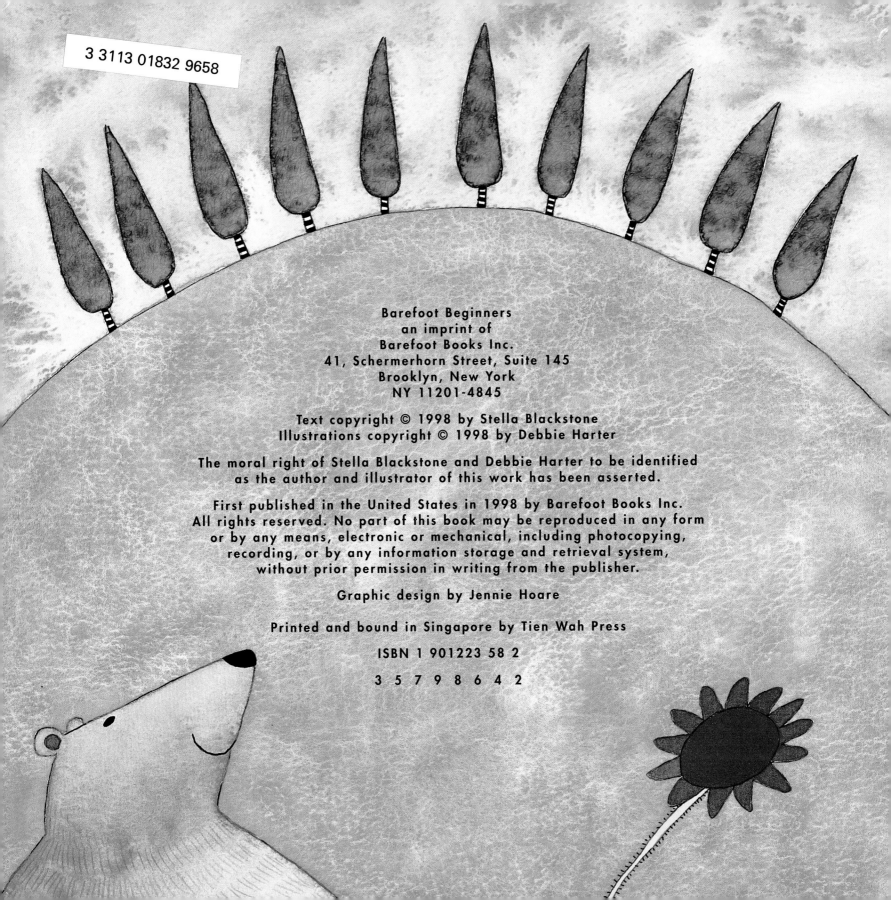

Barefoot Beginners
an imprint of
Barefoot Books Inc.
41, Schermerhorn Street, Suite 145
Brooklyn, New York
NY 11201-4845

Graphic design by Jennie Hoare

Printed and bound in Singapore by Tien Wah Press

ISBN 1 901223 58 2

3 5 7 9 8 6 4 2